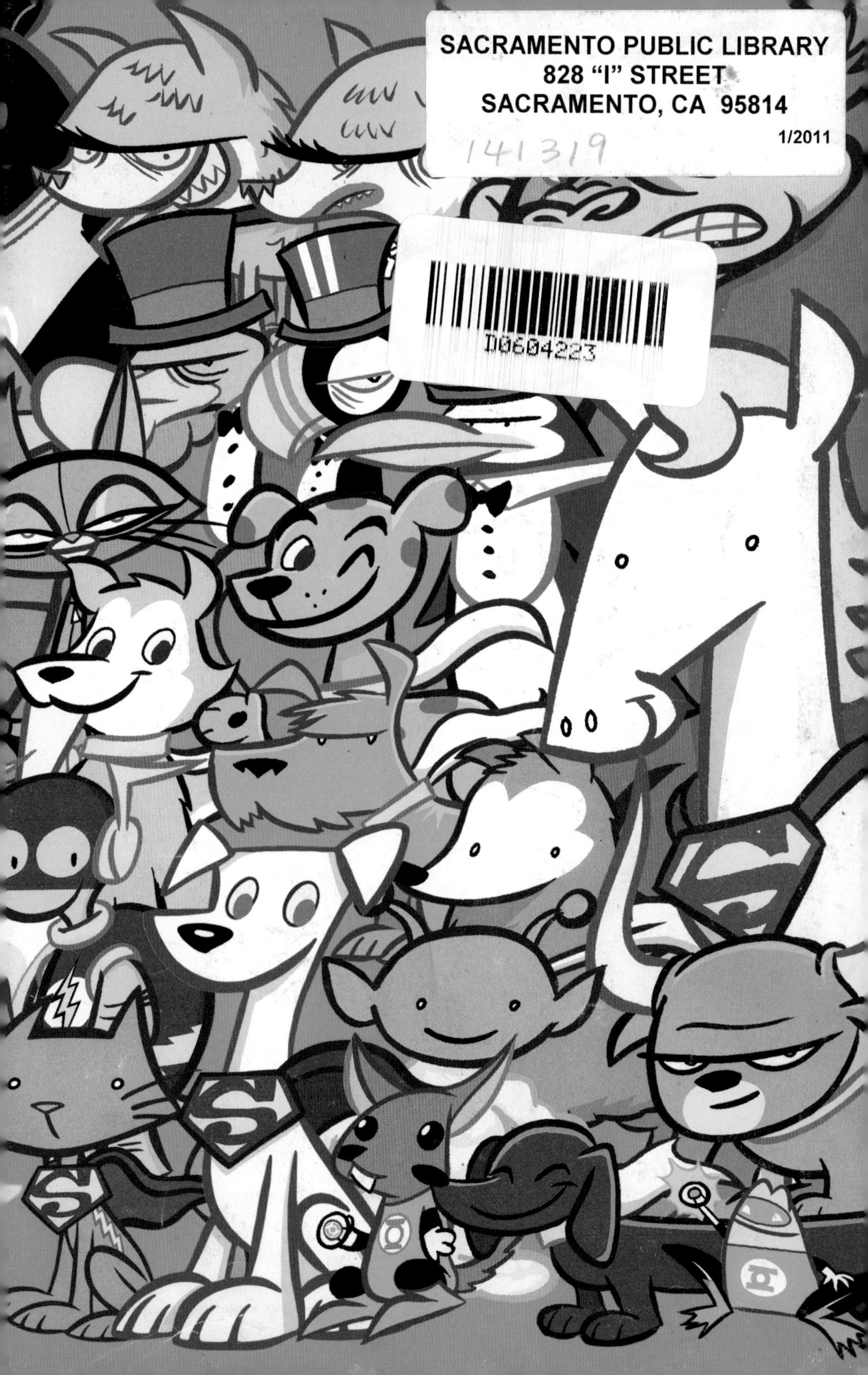

DC™

SUPER-PETS!

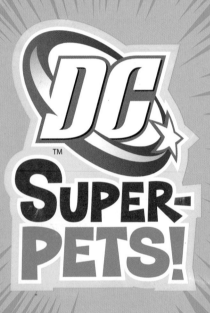

by
Jane Mason

SUPER HERO
SPLASH DOWN

illustrated by
Art Baltazar

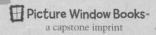
Picture Window Books™
a capstone imprint

Starring...

B'DG
THE GREEN LANTERN!

DEX-STARR
THE RED LANTERN!

SINESTRO DOG CORPS
THE YELLOW LANTERNS!

ROLF!

PRONTO!

SNORRT!

WHOOSH!

GLOMULUS
THE ORANGE LANTERN!

TABLE OF CONTENTS!

GREEN LANTERN CORPS
RING COMPUTER

SUPER-PET HERO FILE 008:

B'DG
Green Lantern,
Sector 1014

Power Ring:

- Creates anything imaginable

- Flight

- Force fields

Super Hero Pal:
HAL JORDAN
Green Lantern, Sector 2814

Species: Space Chipmunk

Place of Birth: H'lvenite

Age: Unknown

Favorite Food:
Ch'ps and salsa

Bio: Like all members of the Green Lantern Corps, B'dg was chosen to protect an area of space from evil. He is pals with fellow Green Lantern Hal Jordan — not his pet!

Chapter 1

WATER PARK RIVALS

"This is the life!" B'dg exclaimed.

The chipmunk-like alien leaned back on his beach towel. He took a sip of his almond smoothie. **SLURP!** He was hanging out at one of his favorite places — the Waves O' Fun water park.

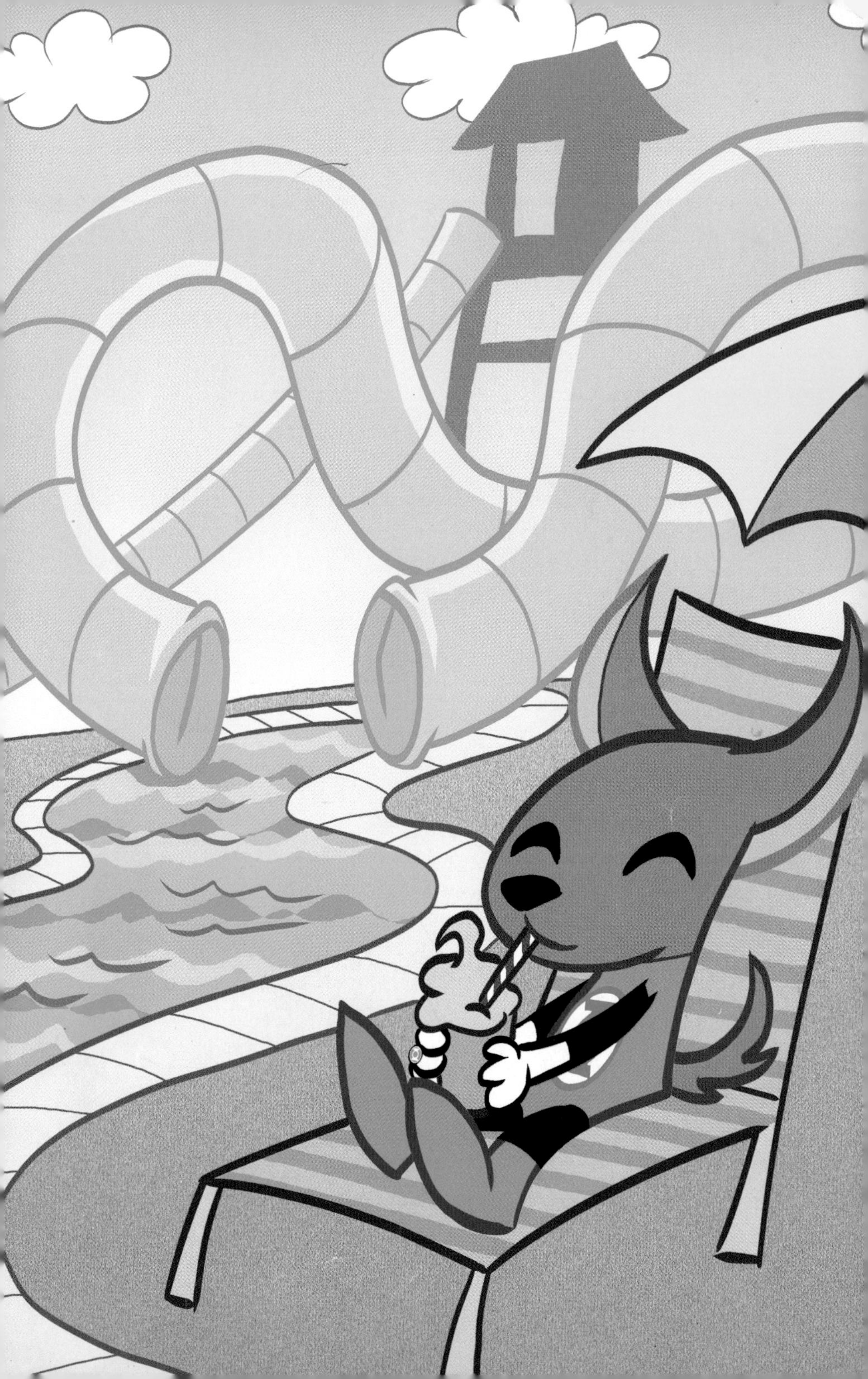

B'dg was a member of the Green Lantern Corps. He spent most of his time protecting outer space. Even with the help of his power ring, the task wasn't easy! He needed an afternoon off.

MUNCH! MUNCH!

B'dg nibbled on his straw. He took in the sights. All around him people laughed and enjoyed the sun. Kids splashed in the pools and sped down water slides. It was perfect.

Across the grassy lawn, people lined up to try to cross the lily pad path. But the lily pads were wobbly! Staying balanced was hard work.

SPA-LOOSH!

Children fell into the cool water.

"I think I'd better show them how it's done," B'dg said, getting to his feet.

He bounced across the lawn. Then suddenly, B'dg skidded to a stop. *No!* he thought. *It can't be him!*

Dex-Starr, a feline Red Lantern, sat at the edge of the pool. Red Lanterns got their power from anger. Dex-Starr was one grumpy kitty. Even at Waves O' Fun, he was scowling. His tail twitched angrily, making his power ring swing.

"Hello, Dex," B'dg said, running

over. "Are you enjoying the sunshine?"

Dex's tail twitched angrily again.

"You're not still mad about the

time I wrapped your tail around the

lifeguard chair, are you?" B'dg asked.

B'dg gave Dex a little shove. The super hero didn't know his own strength. Dex was thrown off balance. He fell into the pool!

"**Whoops!**" B'dg said. He took a step back to avoid getting splashed.

 Dex-Starr howled.

B'dg heard the Red Lantern's cries before the cat's head broke the surface. Dex yowled and pawed at the water.

"Want a paw?" B'dg asked.

Dex's eyes narrowed to slits. **He let out a long, low hiss.**

B'dg backed away slowly. When Dex stepped out of the water, he was soaked. With his fur all wet, the angry cat looked like a skinny skeleton.

"Check out the soaked kitty cat!" a boy called out, pointing.

"Looks like a wet rat!" cried another.

Several people started to laugh.

 Dex cried. His tail flicked madly. Then a red beam of light shot out from his ring. It sizzled in the pool water.

He took a flying leap at B'dg. **The chase was on!**

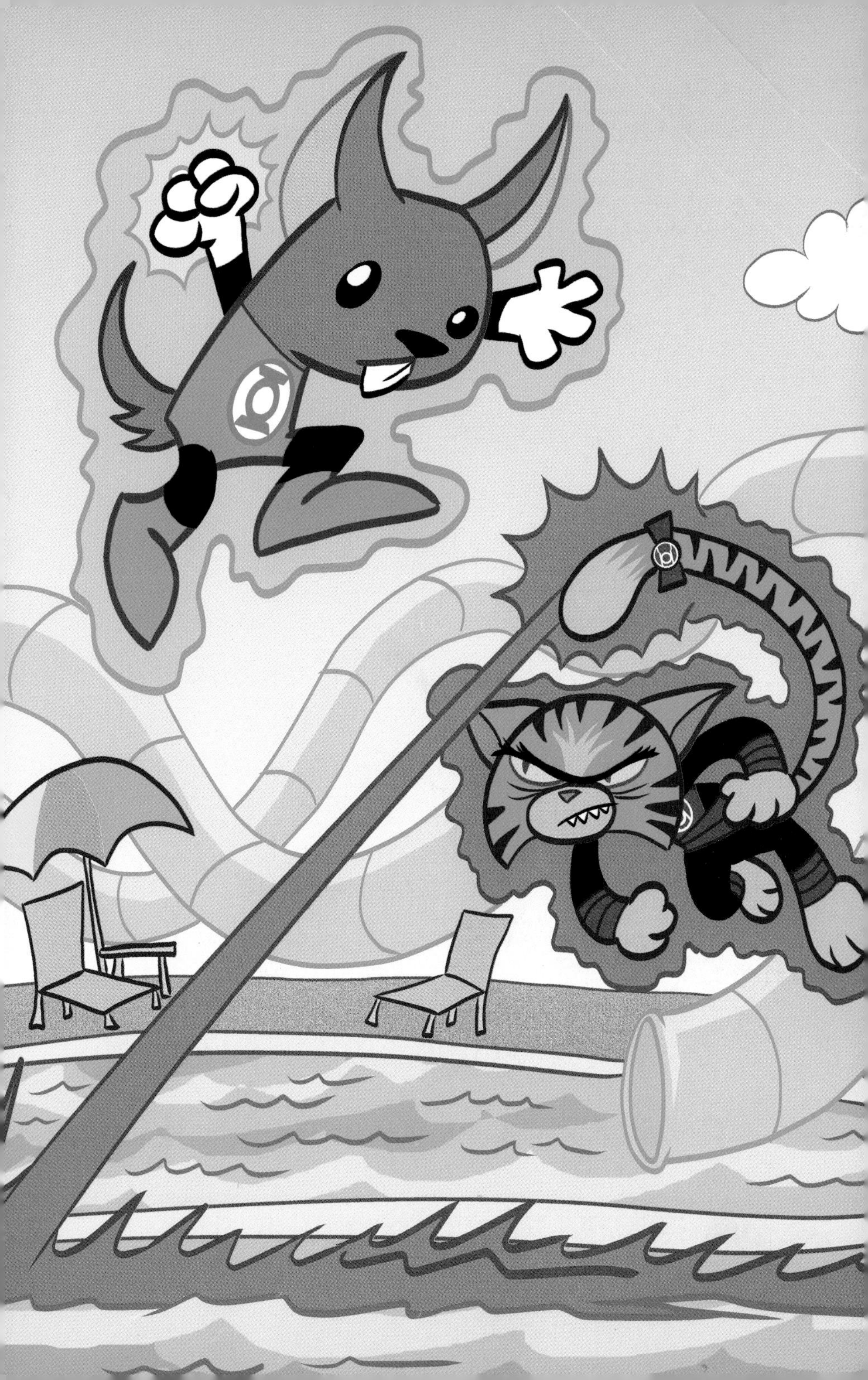

Chapter 2

SPACE CHASE

B'dg leaped into the air. He landed on top of Toboggan Falls, a giant water slide. No sooner had he landed than Dex appeared behind him.

B'dg grabbed a raft from a lifeguard. **"Thanks!"** he called out. He hopped aboard and zoomed down the slide.

Dex's eyes burned with anger. He took a raft out of a little girl's hands. He followed after B'dg. **FWOOSH!**

Soon the rivals were neck and neck. Dex lashed out with a sharp claw. He poked a hole in B'dg's raft. **POP!**

The raft shriveled beneath B'dg.

Water seeped up around his furry legs.

"Thanks for cooling me off!" he said,

slowing to a stop on the slide.

"I'll get you yet!" Dex shouted. His

raft shot past B'dg and quickly came to

the end of the ride.

The evil cat landed in a pool of water

for a second time. B'dg chuckled to

himself. He slid slowly toward the pool.

SPLASH!

B'dg landed at the bottom, taking a cooling dunk in the water. *How refreshing!* he thought.

A moment later, the water around him turned red. It swirled madly. Dex had used the power of his red ring to create an underwater tornado.

FWOOOSH!

"How's that for refreshing?" Dex-Starr hissed from the side of the pool.

The whirlpool spun faster. B'dg could barely breathe. He focused on his ring and imagined a bubble.

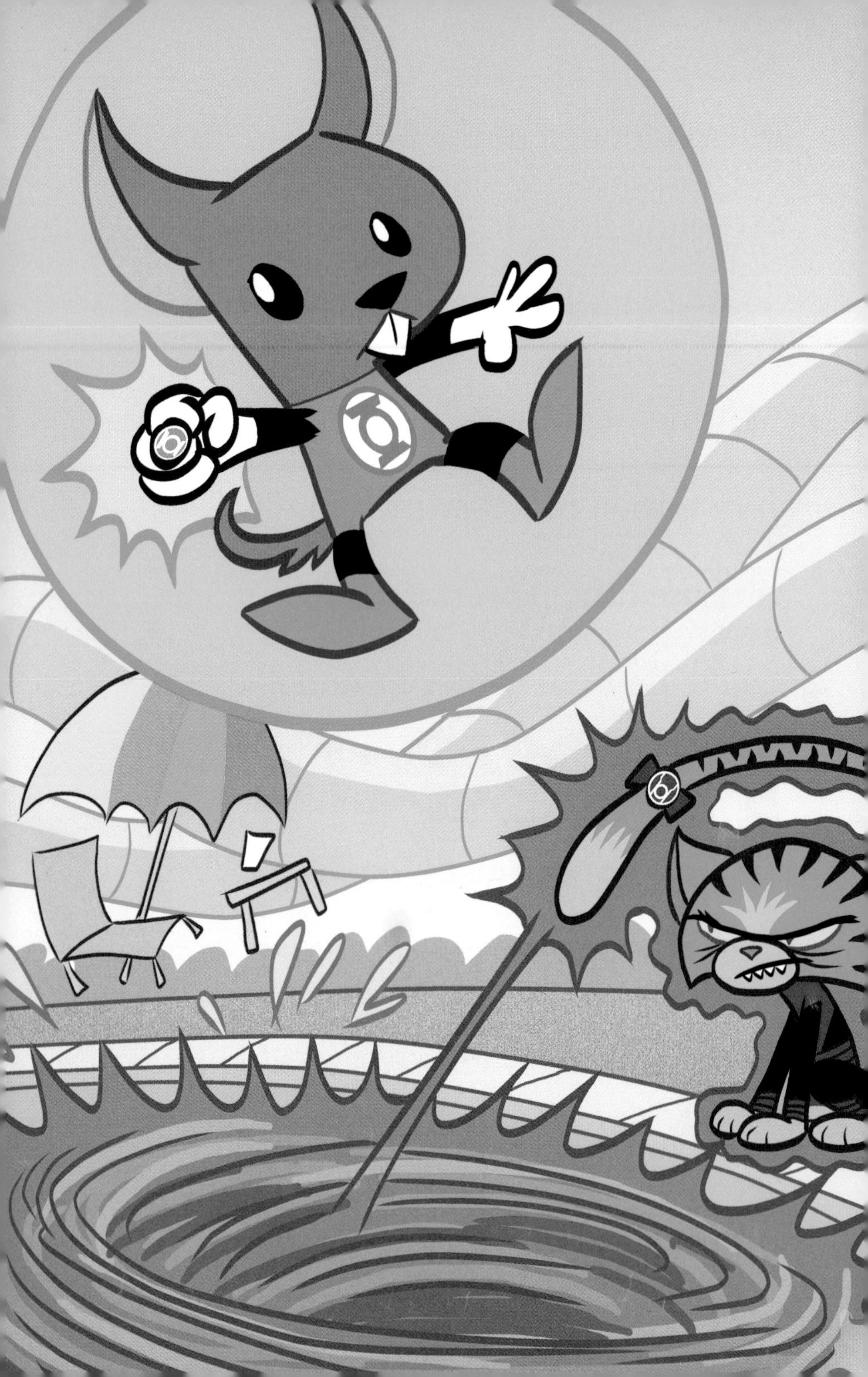

BLUURRRP!

A second later, a balloon of air appeared all around him. It carried the Green Lantern back to the pool's edge.

"**Ha-ha!**" B'dg laughed.

"**You can't escape me!**" Dex shouted back at him.

B'dg skipped across the inner tubes floating along the nearby river of water. "Excuse me! Pardon me!" he told the park guests as he hopped over them.

"**Reeeoowww!**" Dex howled. The

angry cat swished his tail. A red ray

shot out of his ring.

KA-BLAMO!

The beam hit B'dg. It sent him flying

through the air.

"**Wee!**" B'dg cried, enjoying the ride.

WHUMP! The Green Lantern
landed safely on the lily pad path.

Looking around, he smiled. *Now I can show these folks what balance looks like!* he thought.

"**Destroy his path!**" Dex screamed from behind.

BZZZZZT!!

The lily pad floating in front of B'dg exploded. Pieces of green plastic flew in every direction.

"Hey!" a little boy cried. "That kitten blew up the lily pad!"

Thinking fast, B'dg leaped into the air. He pointed his ring at the empty space. He imagined a new lily pad in its place. In half a second, a glowing green pad appeared. **WOOOSH!** B'dg flew through the air, right over the deep pool. **"It's been fun, but I'm outta here!"** he called to Dex.

B'dg landed on the high dive. Then he took two giant jumps. He launched himself into the sky. **BOING!**

"Hissssssssss!" B'dg heard Dex's

cry of rage as he flew through a patch

of clouds. He didn't look back.

B'dg focused on his ring and

imagined he was a rocket. Up, up, up,

he flew.

The alien chipmunk soared away from Earth and into space. All around him stars twinkled and planets spun. A comet zoomed by as he got closer and closer to the sun. It felt good to be out here again.

Then suddenly, B'dg felt something tug him from behind. YOINK!

The Green Lantern looked over his shoulder. He saw a red band of light beaming off Dex-Starr's tail. In another second, he would be pulled toward the evil cat.

Sheesh! he thought. *Can't this kitty take a joke?*

B'dg was done fooling around. He didn't want to fight Dex. The chase wasn't fun anymore. Enough was enough. He stared hard at his ring.

BZZT! A ray of green light smashed against the ray of red.

BZZZZZT!

BZZZZZZT!

The beams clashed against each other again and again.

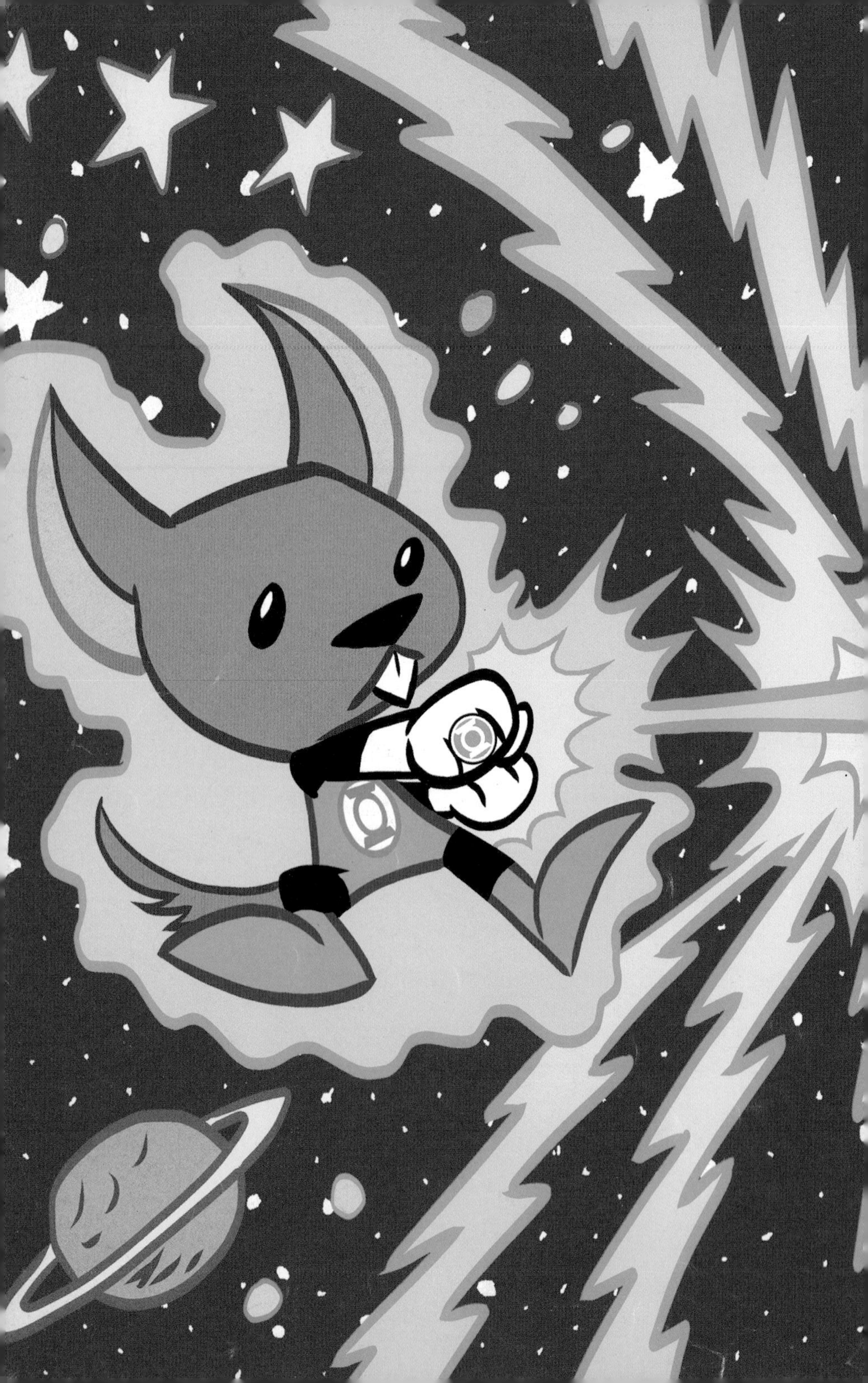

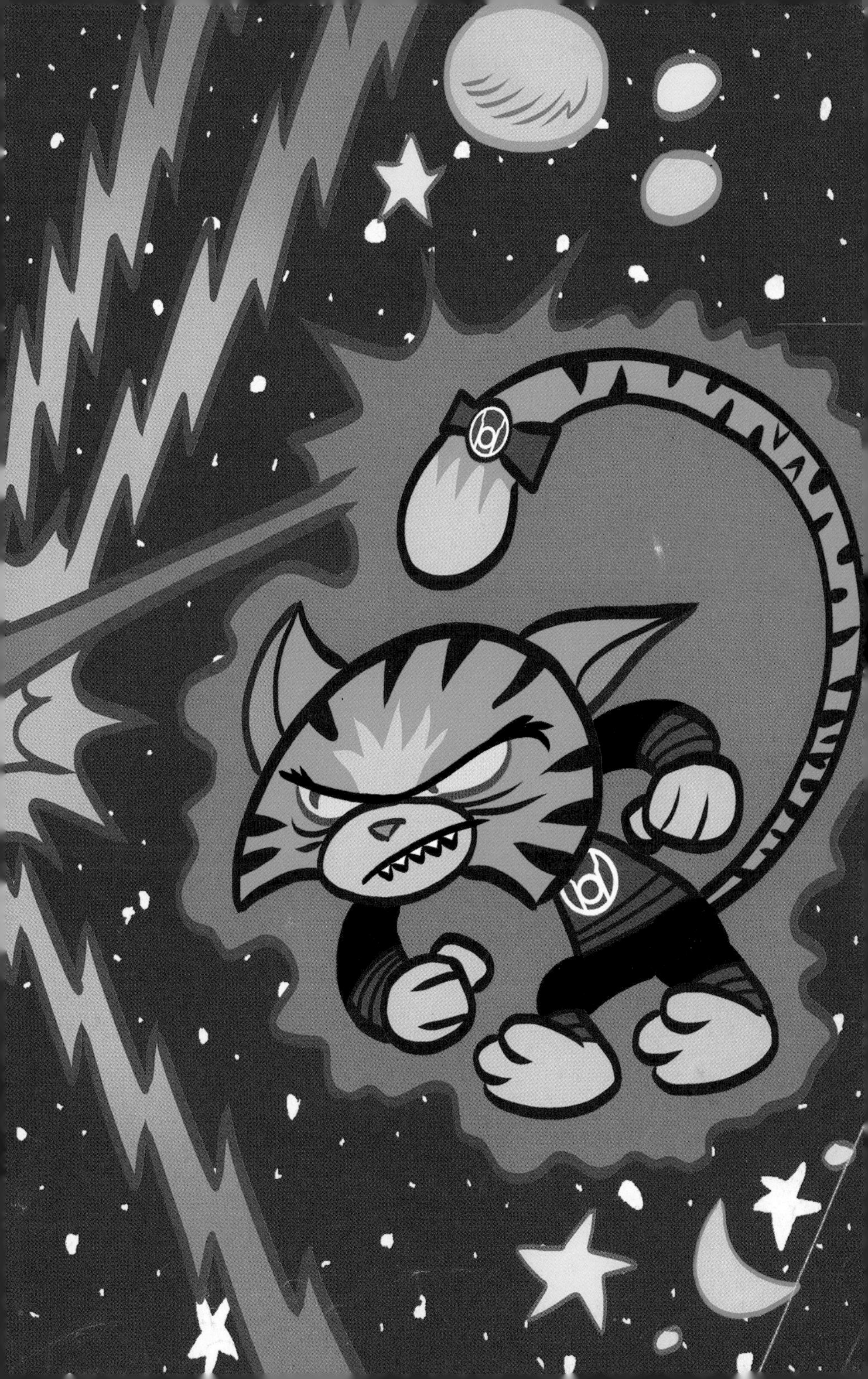

"Ooof!" B'dg and Dex grunted with the effort. B'dg's arm began to tire. He got sweaty. The rivals were close to the sun, and it was getting hot!

B'dg wouldn't give up. "It was an accident!" he shouted at Dex.

The power ring rays clashed again, sending sparks flying. It looked like outer space fireworks!

Then suddenly, a chorus of barks came from behind.

B'dg groaned. Their little battle

had gotten the attention of the

Sinestro Dog Corps, a yellow pack of

troublemaking mutts.

"Nice little light show," growled a

voice. **RUFF! RUFF!**

B'dg did not let the dogs distract him. He focused on his ring again. He imagined his green beam blowing out the red beam as if it were a candle. **"I didn't mean to push you into the pool, Dex!"** he shouted.

"Pool?" Snorrt, one of the dogs, asked. **"What pool?"** His tongue slobbered between his yellow teeth.

"You expect me to believe that?" Dex-Starr yowled at B'dg. "Every time you're at Waves O' Fun water park, you're out to get me!"

"Waves O' Fun!"

a dog named

Pronto howled.

"You hear that,

boys?" Rolf, the

lead dog, growled.

"Waves O' Fun!"

"Sounds like a cool place to me,"

Snorrt said.

WOOF! WOOF! WOOF!

"Let's go for a dip, boys!" one of the

dogs howled. "And maybe stir up a

wave while we're there."

B’dg overheard the yowling dogs. “Did you hear that?” he asked Dex.

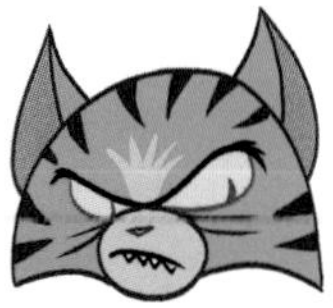

Dex’s tail flicked. **“Sinestro Dog Corps in the water park?”** he said. “They’d do a lot worse than push a kitty into the pool!” He whirled around, swinging his ring’s red ray away from B’dg. “Let’s stop ’em!”

BZZZZZT!!

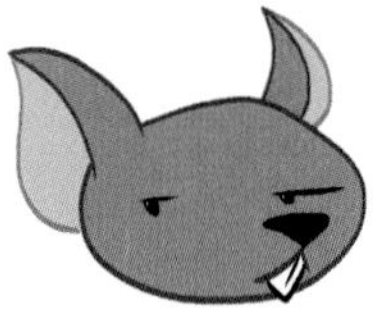

“Working together, our rings should do the trick!” B’dg replied as they turned to face the pack of yellow pups.

Chapter 3

FRIENDS AND ENEMIES

B'dg looked around. The dogs were huddled together a few yards away. They argued about who should lead the way to Waves O' Fun.

"I'm the leader!" Rolf growled.

"Last time you led us to Earth we got lost!" Pronto shouted.

B'dg imagined a bunch of bones.
They appeared from his ring. He tossed
them into the doggie huddle.

The dogs jumped on the snack.
Snarls and grunts could be heard for
space miles. B'dg thought that the
snack would buy enough time to think
of a real plan. But five seconds later,
the dogs were already licking their lips.

**"Come on, boys! Let's go make
some waves!"** Rolf barked. He took off
toward Earth and Waves O' Fun.

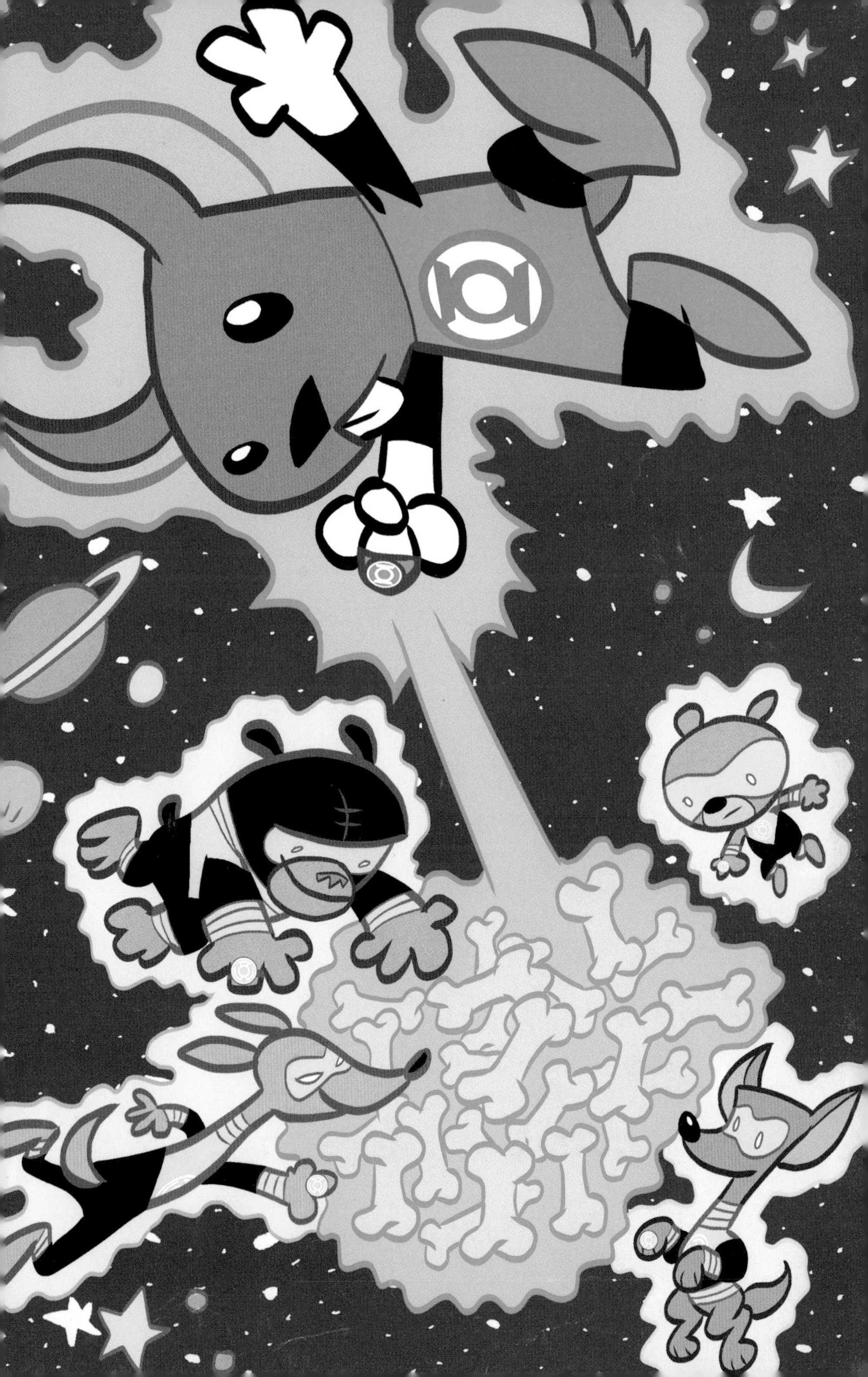

"Thanks for the snack, pet!"

Snorrt called over his shoulder as the

pack of dogs took off.

"I am not a pet!"

B'dg shouted. "I'm a Green Lantern!"

"Reowww!" Dex chased after them.

The evil cat's red beam shot through the blackness of space. His anger made the beam grow longer and longer. Soon, it was in front of the pack of nasty dogs.

Dex swung his tail. He made his red ray zigzag across the galaxy. **"Here, doggies,"** he said.

BZZZT! BZZZT!

Rolf began to follow the lights. The pack of Sinestro Dogs followed.

"Lead them to Nupe!" B'dg said.

Nupe was a tiny moon close the sun. It had really, really strong gravity. If they could get the dogs close enough, they'd get stuck there like magnets.

Dex-Starr swung his tail in a giant arc. He turned the dogs away from Earth and toward Nupe.

HOWWWLLL!

The dogs howled as they followed the red light. Suddenly, they stopped.

"Rolf, you're gettin' us lost again!" Pronto growled.

The dogs were on to them! B'dg stared down at his ring. He imagined that he was in a kitchen filled with roasting meat. He focused on the smell and put it into his ring. Then he flew right into Dex's red beam and sprinkled the delicious odor out in front of the dogs.

The dogs' noses twitched in the air.

"Roast meat!" B'dg whispered to the hounds.

"My meat!" Pronto cried, taking off after the smell.

"Mine! Mine!" the others barked.

The smell of the meat got stronger and stronger. Soon the dogs were racing toward Nupe.

"My meat! No! Mine!" they shouted. B'dg flung that last bit of roasted meat odor toward the dogs. He grinned as they got caught in Nupe's gravity.

They were stuck in an invisible net.

Dex-Starr chuckled to himself. He pulled the red beam back into his ring.

"Dex, did I just hear you laugh?" B'dg asked.

Dex narrowed his yellow eyes. "Of course not," he said. His tail twitched.

B'dg smiled. The pesky Sinestro Dogs would not be causing trouble for a while. And Dex-Starr was not mad at him — at least not at the moment.

"Waves O' Fun, here we come," B'dg called. He and Dex took off toward Earth. "I can show you how to cross the lily pads."

"You mean I can show *you* how to cross the lily pads," Dex meowed.

They soared past planets and stars and through Earth's atmosphere.

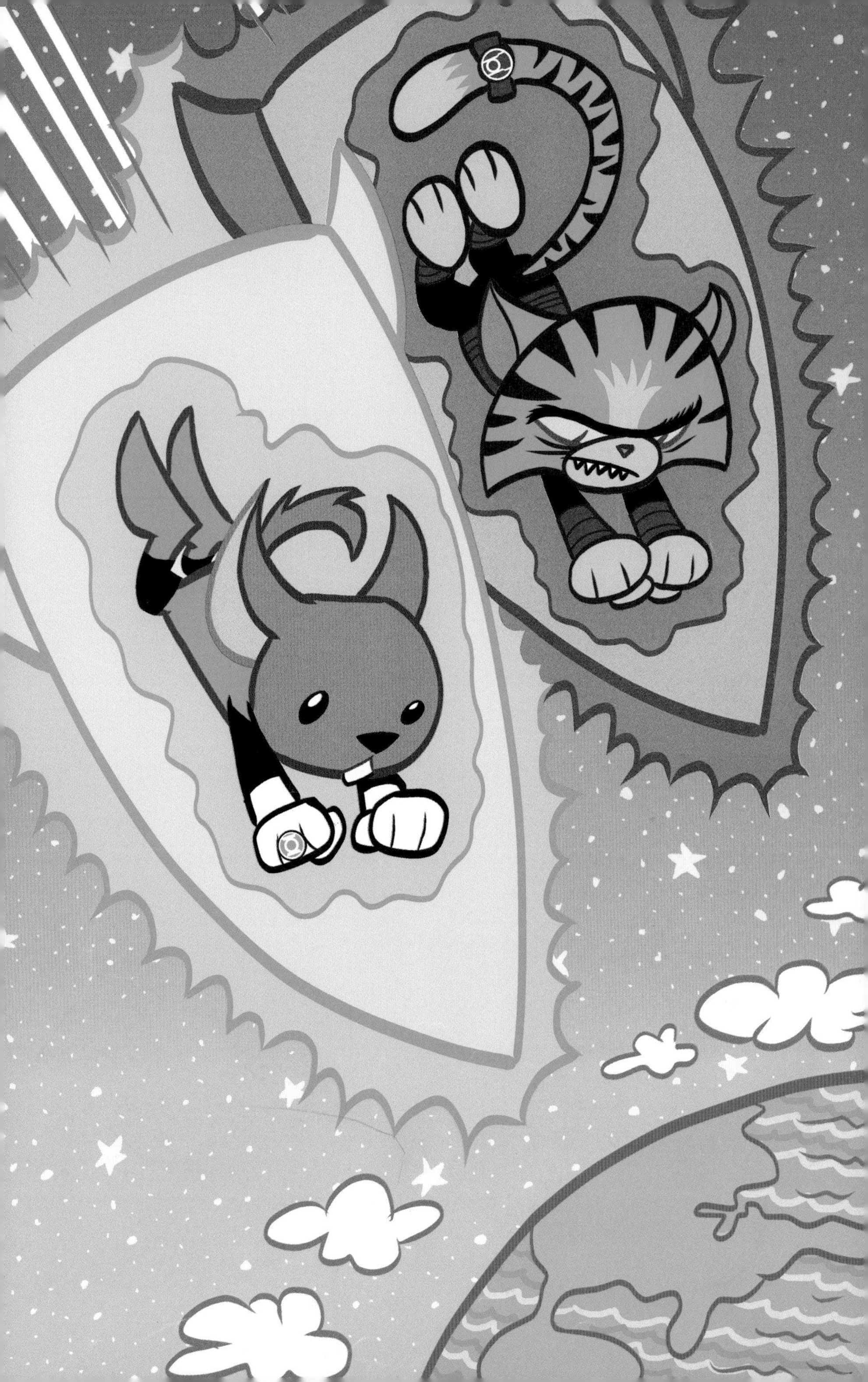

Soon they were zooming through puffy white clouds and touching down at Waves O' Fun.

When his paws hit the ground, B'dg could tell that something was wrong. Nobody was in the water. Lifeguards were blowing their whistles. People were running and shrieking. And there was a strange orange glow coming from one of the pools.

B'dg scanned the lily pads and saw the problem.

Glomulus, the disgusting Orange Lantern, was sitting in the center lily pad next to a giant heap of junk food.

"Where'd he come from?" B'dg said, pointing at the orange blob gobbling hot dogs and slurping sodas.

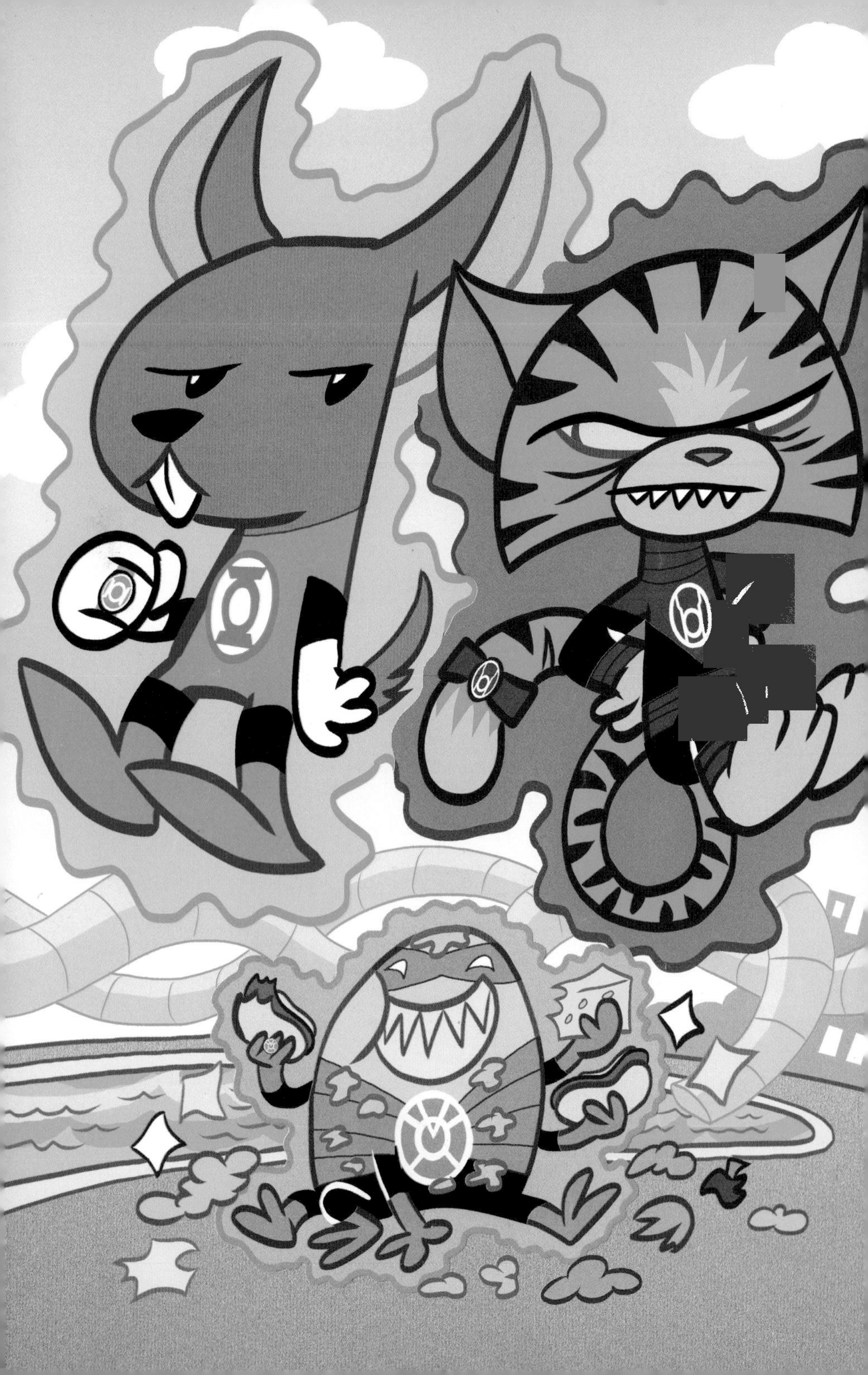

BLURRRRP!

Glomulus let out a loud burp.

"If it's not one Corps, it's another!"
Dex said. **"Those greedy Orange
Lanterns ruin everyone else's fun."**

"No kidding," B'dg agreed. He knew
Glomulus would be hard to get rid of.

"Oh boy," B'dg said to Dex-Starr.
**"Suddenly, the Sinestro Dogs don't
seem so bad."**

KNOW YOUR

Krypto

Streaky

Beppo

Comet

Ace

Jumpa

Whatzit

B'dg

Storm

Topo

Ark

Hoppy

Paw Pooch

Bull Dog

Chameleon
Collie

Hot Dog

Aw yeah,
**HERO
PETS!**

Tail Terrier

Tusky
Husky

SUPER-PETS!

Ignatius

Chauncey

Crackers

Giggles

Artie Puffin

Griff

Waddles

Rozz

Dex-Starr

Glomulus

Misty

Sneezers

Whoosh

Pronto

Snorrt

Rolf

Squealer

Kajunn

Aw yeah, **VILLAIN PETS!**

AW YEAH, JOKES!

Why did the cat run from the tree?

Why?

It was afraid of the bark!

How do you catch a space chipmunk?

Dunno.

Climb a tree and act NUTS!

What is a cat's favorite sport?

Tell me.

Hairball!

WORD POWER!

balance (BAL-uhnss)—the ability to keep steady and not fall over

distract (diss-TRAKT)—weaken a person's focus on someone or something

focused (FOH-kuhssd)—concentrated on someone or something

gravity (GRAV-uh-tee)—the force that pulls things down toward the surface of Earth

imagined (i-MAJ-uhnd)—pictured something in your mind

rival (RYE-vuhl)—someone you are competing against

MEET THE AUTHOR!

Jane Mason

Jane Mason is no super hero, but having three kids sometimes makes her wish she had superpowers. Jane has written children's books for more than fifteen years and hopes to continue doing so for fifty more. She makes her home in Oakland, California, with her husband, three children, their dog, and a gecko.

MEET THE ILLUSTRATOR!

Eisner Award-winner Art Baltazar

Art Baltazar is a cartoonist machine from the heart of Chicago! He defines cartoons and comics not only as an art style, but as a way of life. Currently, Art is the creative force behind *The New York Times* best-selling, Eisner Award-winning, DC Comics series Tiny Titans and the co-writer for *Billy Batson and the Magic of SHAZAM!* Art is living the dream! He draws comics and never has to leave the house. He lives with his lovely wife, Rose, big boy Sonny, little boy Gordon, and little girl Audrey. Right on!

Art Baltazar says:

Read all of the DC SUPER-PETS stories today!

⊞ Picture Window Books™

Published in 2011
A Capstone Imprint
151 Good Counsel Drive, P.O. Box 669
Mankato, Minnesota 56002
www.capstonepub.com

Cataloging-in-Publication Data is available at the
Library of Congress website.

ISBN: 978-1-4048-6357-6 (library binding)
ISBN: 978-1-4048-6624-9 (paperback)

Summary: B'dg's day in the sun is anything
but fun when the villain Dex-Starr shows
up. But soon, these foes discover a common
enemy . . . the Sinestro Dog Corps! If the
Lantern rivals can't unite, their favorite
water park might become a mutt puddle.

Art Director & Designer: Bob Lentz
Editor: Donald Lemke
Production Specialist: Michelle Biedscheid
Creative Director: Heather Kindseth
Editorial Director: Michael Dahl
Publisher: Lori Benton

Printed in the United States of America
in Stevens Point, Wisconsin.
092010   005934WZS11

DC™ SUPER-PETS!

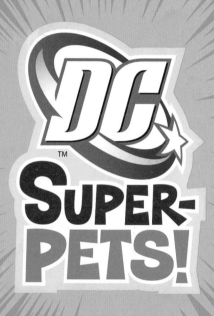

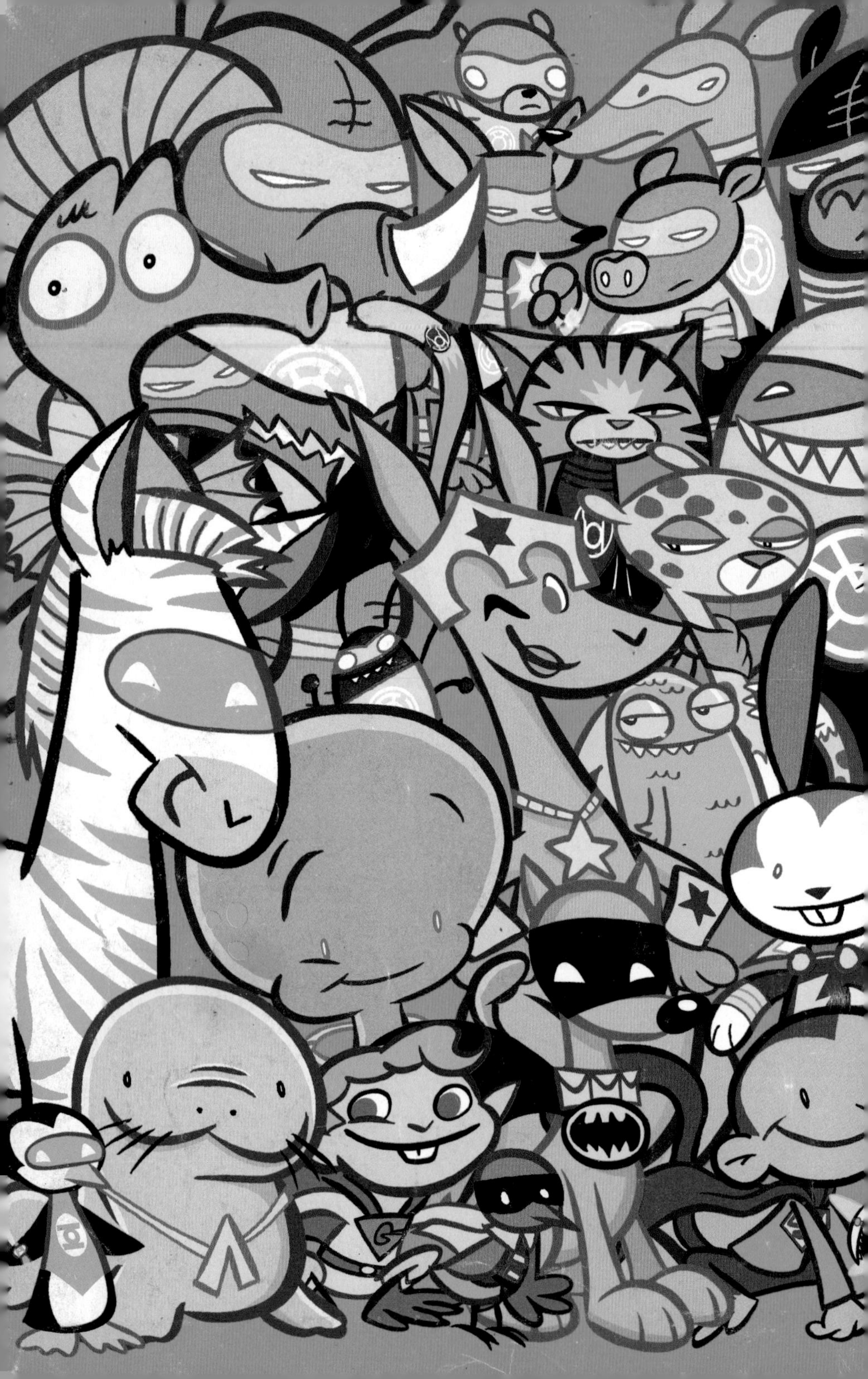